For children ages 3-7

SMARTY
The Adventurous Fly
Learns Not to Wander Too Far from Home

Regal Books

A Division of GL Publications
Ventura, California U.S.A.

Ethel Barrett
Clay art by David Gaddy

Published by Regal Books
A Division of GL Publications
Ventura, California 93006
Printed in U.S.A.

Library of Congress Cataloging-in-Publication Date applied for

Rights for publishing this book in other languages are contracted by Gospel Literature International
(GLINT) foundation. GLINT also provides technical help for the adaptation, translation, and
publishing of Bible study resources and books in scores of languages worldwide. For further
information, contact GLINT, Post Office Box 488, Rosemead, California, 91770, U.S.A., or the
publisher.

This is a story of a little fly
who was very, very SMART. His name was Sam, but
he was so smart that all his relatives
and all his friends nicknamed him SMARTY.

He knew just when to fly away
before anybody swatted him.
So, by the time the swatter landed,
he was off and aw-a-a-ay.
Now Smarty was not only very, very smart,
but he was also very, very adventurous.
He loved to fly where none of his friends
dared to go.

He would even fly way
out to the airport.
He loved to look at the great big planes.
He would watch them take off.
And then watch them zoom up into the air
until they finally disappeared.
And, it might have ended right there
except that one day—Smarty got
too smart for his own good.

It was the day he saw that big plane
on the ground—and the door was open!
Smarty saw his chance.
He flew right up to that plane.
And through the open door and
landed on the back of a seat!
But before he could catch his breath,
another fly flew in and landed right beside him.
It was his cousin COZY.

Sam's antennas stood up straight.

"Cozy! What are you doing here?"

"I followed you in," Cozy said.

"Smarty, you've got to get off this plane.

This plane is nonstop to DENVER."

"I don't care, Cozy.

I just want ADVENTURE."

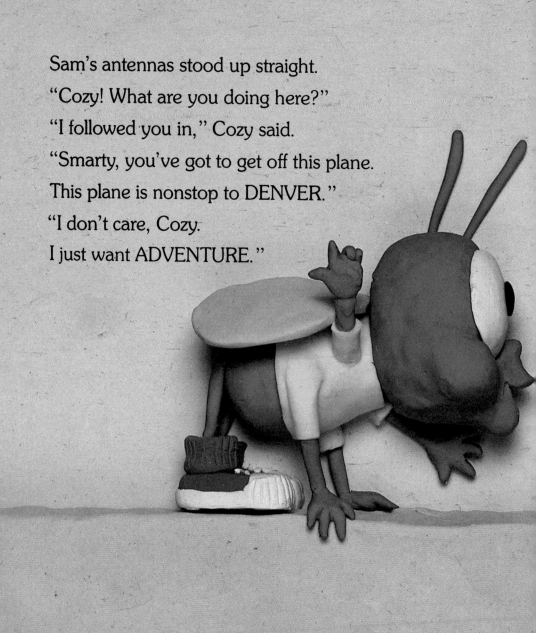

"But it's SNOWING in Denver, Smarty," Cozy said.
"They're having a STORM in Denver.
You'll FREEZE to death! And besides,
what will your parents say when their friends
ask them where you are?"
"They'll have to say, 'We don't know.
He got on a nonstop flight to Denver and
he never came back.'"
"Oh, Smarty—please get off the plane with me!"
"No," said Smarty, "I'm going to take this plane
to Denver. I want ADVENTURE!"

So Cozy flew away and out the open door,
and Smarty was left alone on the plane.
Smarty didn't care one bit.
He flew up against the window and looked out
and he flew all over the plane and
inspected all the passengers, and he even lit
on the ceiling and crawled around there for a while.

And when the plane took off and zoomed up into the air,
he knew that his great adventure had begun!

He just zoomed around and visited everybody.

He landed on ladies' hats.

And when the meals were served,

he swooped down and nibbled on the crumbs.

And he was always quick enough to fly away

before anybody swatted him.

And everything was going very well, thank you,

when suddenly—a man's big voice boomed out

all over the plane.

"This is your captain speaking.

Make sure your seat belts are fastened.

We're going to run into some rough weather."

Well, this didn't seem to bother
the passengers one single bit.
It sure scared Smarty, though,
for the plane began to jump up and down—
up and *down*—and
Smarty bounced up and down with it!
Everyplace he tried to fly
he zigged and he zagged
and he tumbled—until he didn't know
whether he was flying rightside up—
or upside down! And then—
What was THAT?!?

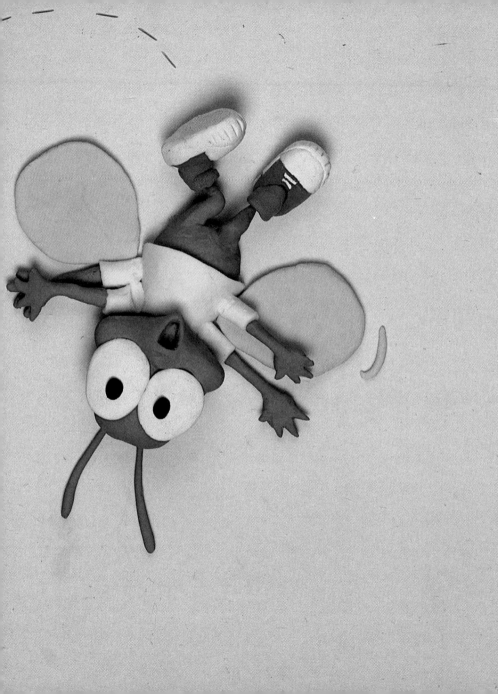

It was a THUNDERSTORM! Ohhhhh!
Smarty managed to find
his way over to a window.
And he clung to the window
and looked out.
He couldn't see a thing.
The rain was coming down hard.
And it was beating
against the window.

Smarty was so frightened, he forgot to hang on,
and the next thing he knew he went tumbling down,
down, down—right into the brim of a lady's hat.
And there he stayed, trembling with fear—
and waited. And waited. It seemed like a long time
before the thunderstorm was gone
and the plane stopped bouncing around.
By this time, Smarty was afraid
to come out.

And it seemed like FOREVER before the plane
finally landed—in DENVER.
Now Smarty got smart again.
He crawled up to the top of the brim of the lady's hat
and took off and started for the open door.
When he got to it—
WHAT WAS THIS?!? It was a fierce snowstorm!
The wind was blowing and the snow was swirling.
Smarty had never even seen snow before—
and he'd never seen a storm like this.
He clung to the side of the door and the wind
blew his wings up like an umbrella turned inside out—
and he shivered and shook like he'd never done before.
For he knew that if he went out into that storm,
he would FREEZE.

It was all he could do to struggle back
into the plane.
He crawled under a seat, shivering, and
there he curled up into a ball and
shivered and shivered.
It was a long time before his wings
thawed out and he could get them
moving again.
And, it seemed like forever before
the big plane turned around again
and headed back to his hometown.

The trip back was smooth and wonderful.
The big plane just sailed along
way up over the clouds, and
all the people enjoyed it very much.
But not Smarty. He couldn't fly very well
and his legs were still wobbly.
He had a hard time just crawling around.
But at last the big plane landed—
right in the very spot
where Smarty's great adventure
had begun and—joy, oh joy!—
there was cousin Cozy to greet him!
Smarty wobbled down the steps
one jump at a time, and
finally fell into Cozy's arms.

"Smarty! Smarty! You're back!" Cozy cried,
"I've been waiting for you.
I knew you'd come back. How was your trip?"
"Oh cousin Cozy, it was AWFUL," Smarty wailed.
"I thought I would *never* get back home again alive."
"Smarty, I *told* you not to run away.
You could have all the adventure
you want right here
in your backyard!"

"I know that now, cousin Cozy."
Smarty was crying now. "And I'll never, *never*
run away again! Let's go home."
As soon as Smarty could get his wings
working again, that's exactly what they did.
And was Smarty ever GLAD
to see his family!

And were THEY ever glad to see him!
And Smarty was as good as his word,
for after all, he was A VERY SMART LITTLE FLY.
He never, NEVER ran away again.
Just like the Bible says, "Be content with what you have"
Hebrews 13:5 (*NIV*). You can *miss out* on the ENJOYMENT
and FUN of what you have, if you keep wanting
something else!